ROCKET BOY

For Finlay and Zoe – and Cosmo the cat!

– Katie

For my grandparents, Jen and Den

– Joe

STRIPES PUBLISHING LIMITED
An imprint of the Little Tiger Group
1 Coda Studios,
189 Munster Road,
London SW6 6AW

First published in Great Britain in 2020

Text copyright © Katie Jennings, 2020
Illustrations copyright © Joe Lillington, 2020

ISBN: 978-1-78895-202-6

A CIP catalogue record for this book
is available from the British Library.

STP/1800/0299/0220

Printed and bound in China.

MIX
Paper from
responsible sources
FSC® C020056

The Forest Stewardship Council® (FSC®) is a global, not-for-profit organization dedicated
to the promotion of responsible forest management worldwide. FSC defines standards based
on agreed principles for responsible forest stewardship that are supported by environmental,
social, and economic stakeholders. To learn more, visit www.fsc.org

2 4 6 8 10 9 7 5 3 1

ROCKET BOY

Katie Jennings and Joe Lillington

LITTLE TIGER
LONDON

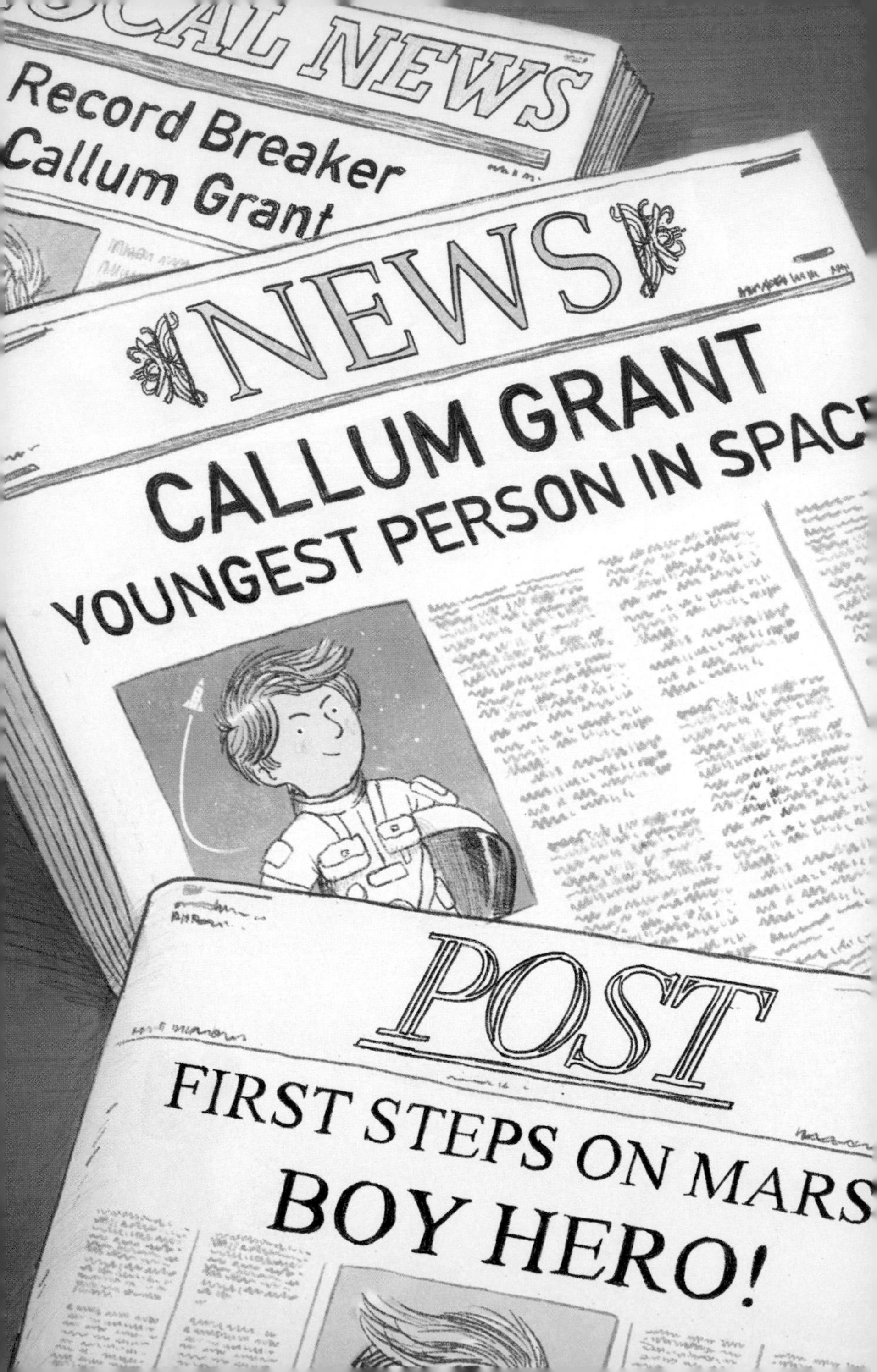
LOCAL NEWS
Record Breaker
Callum Grant
NEWS
CALLUM GRANT
YOUNGEST PERSON IN SPACE
POST
FIRST STEPS ON MARS
BOY HERO!

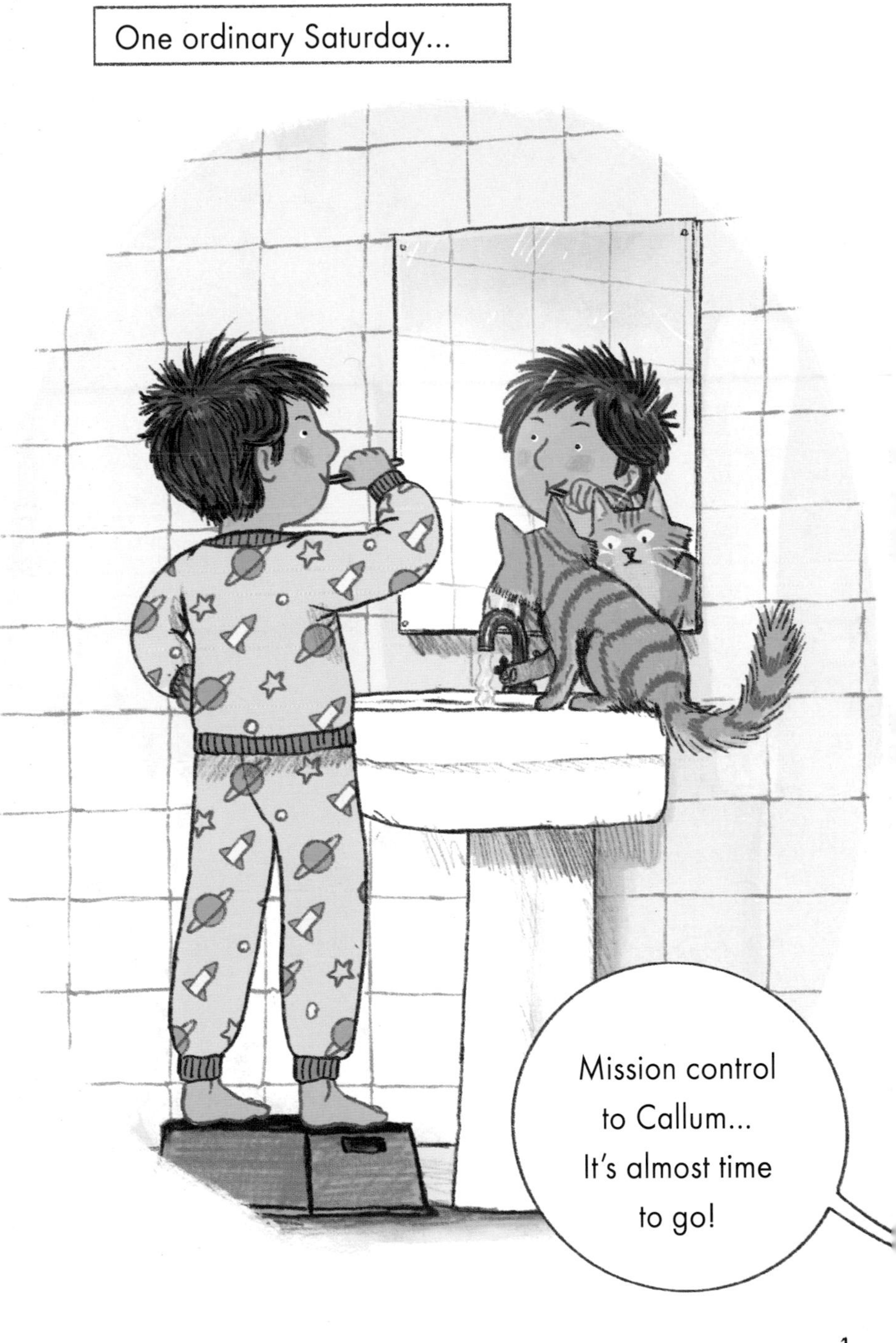
One ordinary Saturday...
Mission control to Callum... It's almost time to go!

"Mum, did you know it takes 1.3 seconds for light to reach us from the moon?"

"I didn't," says Mum. "Counting down to take off. *Five, four, three, two, one—*"

" *Lift off!* "

"Look at that cloud – it's just like the International Space Station."

"Callum Grant, you could find a shooting star in broad daylight!"

"Shooting stars don't exist, Mum. They're actually meteors."

"Would you rather be crushed by a meteorite or sucked into a black hole?"

"Hmm. Let me think..."

"Black hole! Look out! Arrgh! There's no escape..."

Splash!

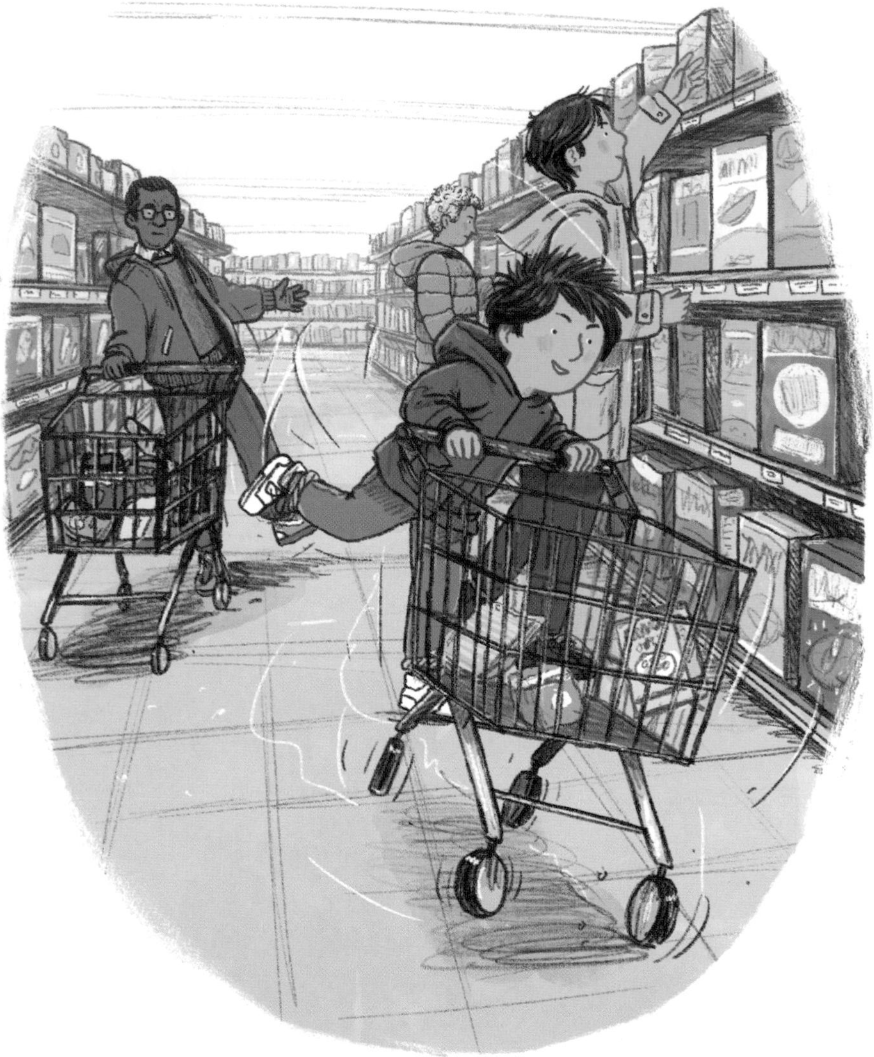

"Right, Callum, we just need broccoli and some carrots."

Callum clutches his throat. "Ugh, not broccoli!"

"Yes, broccoli," says Mum, tossing some into the trolley.

"Mission accomplished!"

"Do you know what colour
sunsets are on Mars, Mum?" asks Callum.

"Eat up. One tiny piece of broccoli
won't kill you," says Mum.

"Stop changing the subject, Mum!
Don't you know the answer?"

"Yellow?"

"Nope!"

"Red?"

"Wrong again!" says Callum. "Martian sunsets are blue. But the sky on Mars is red."

"Fascinating, Cal," says Mum. "Now, eat your—"

Ding dong!

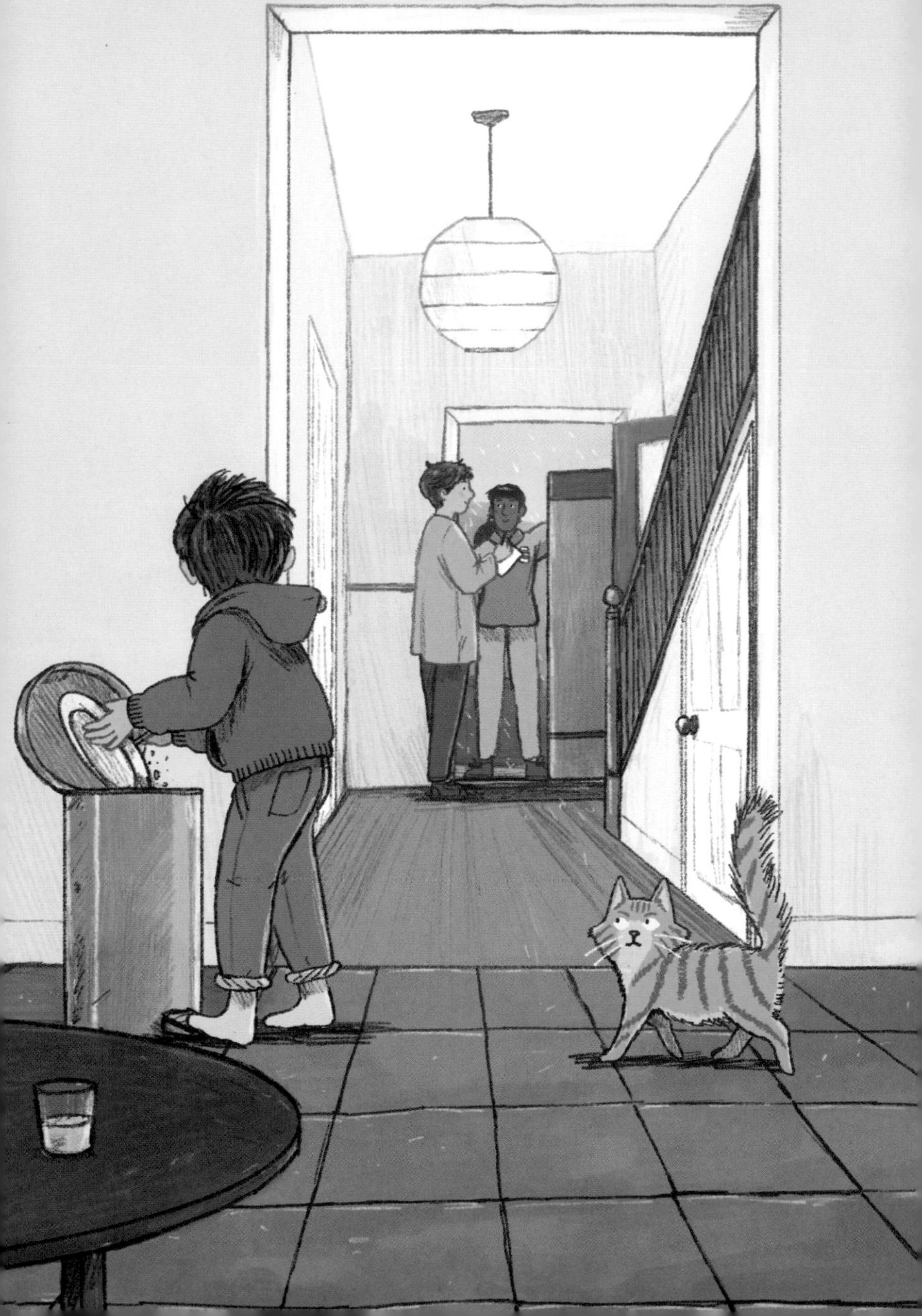

Callum finds Mum in the living room,
opening a giant cardboard box.

"What's in there?" he asks.

"My new desk."

Callum glances over at a second – slightly smaller – box.

"Anything for me?" he says hopefully.

"Not today," says Mum.

Some time later...

"Our trainee astronaut is bearing up well in the G-force simulator..."

"Please don't do that, Cal. I haven't even had the chance to sit on it yet."

"One small

step for a boy,

one giant—"

"Callum, please!" Mum sighs. "I just can't think! Why don't you go and play in your room? You can take the boxes, if you like."

Th-wish. Th-wish.

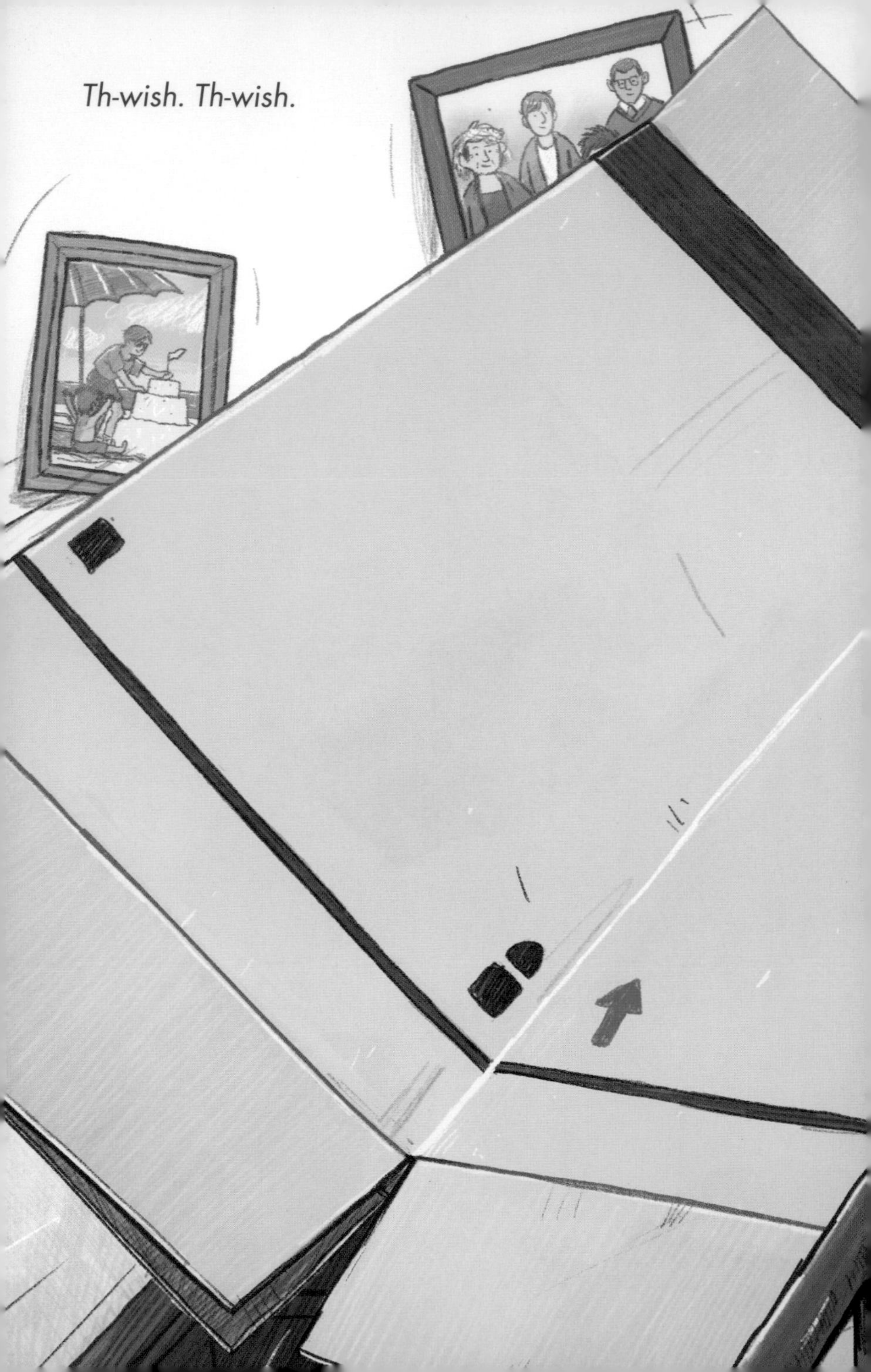

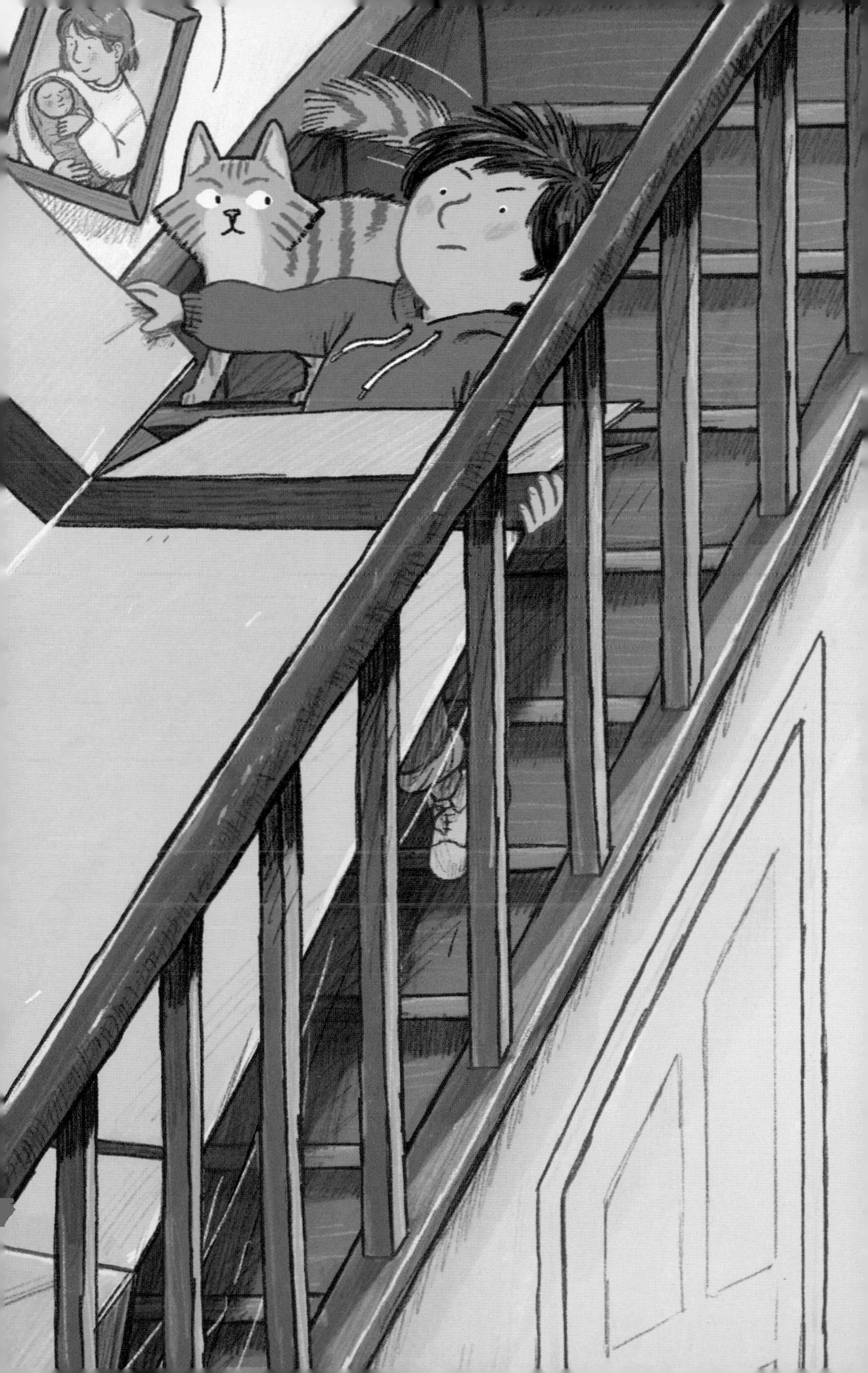

Callum gets out his drawing pad and pencils.

He sketches ... and sketches.

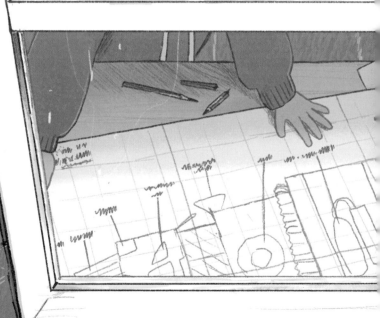

Finally he puts down his pencil and surveys his design.

"Perfect! Now, what do I need?"

Callum hurries downstairs.
*Mum won't mind if I
borrow a few things,*
he tells himself.

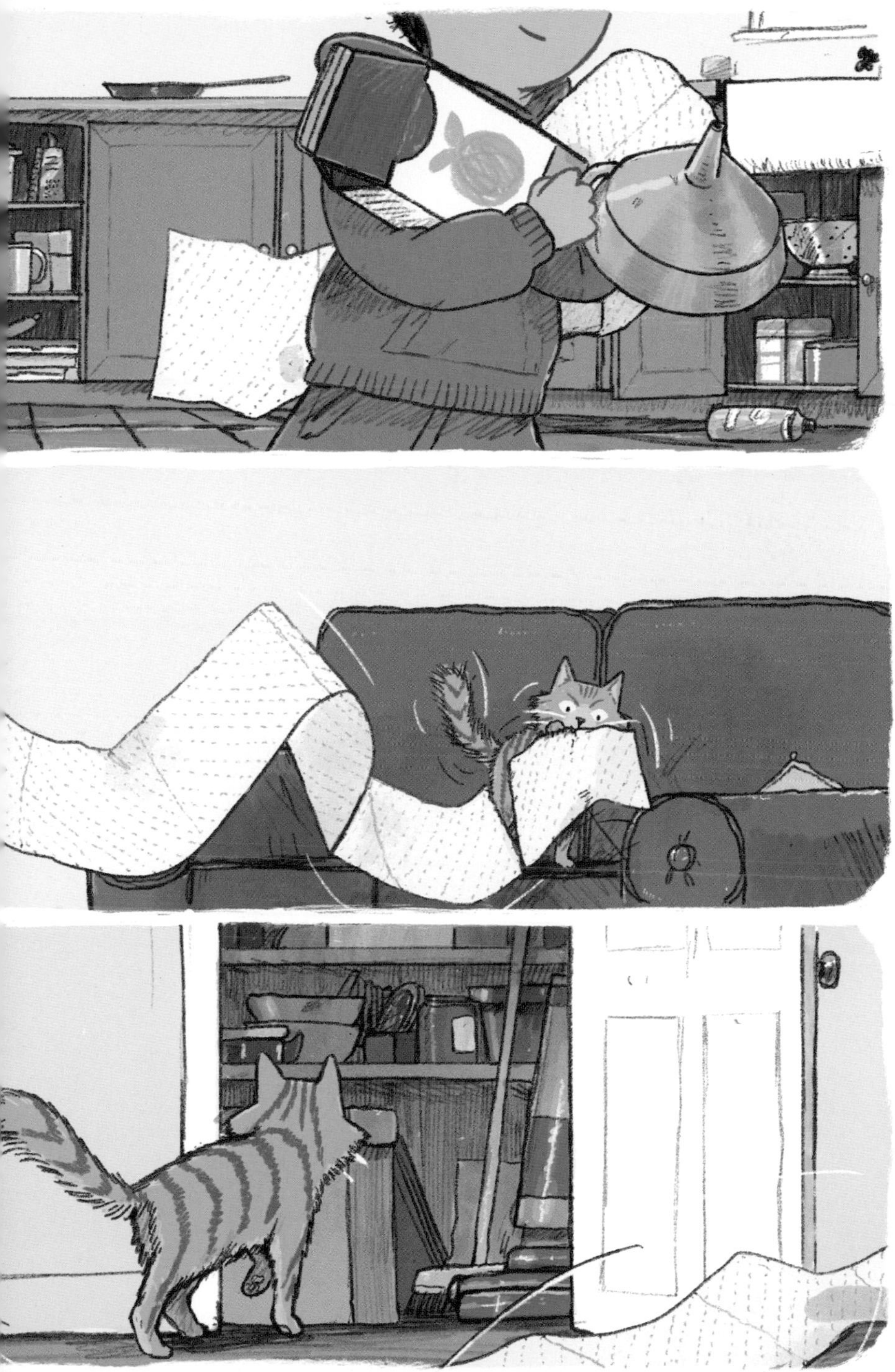

"Mum, can I have this?"

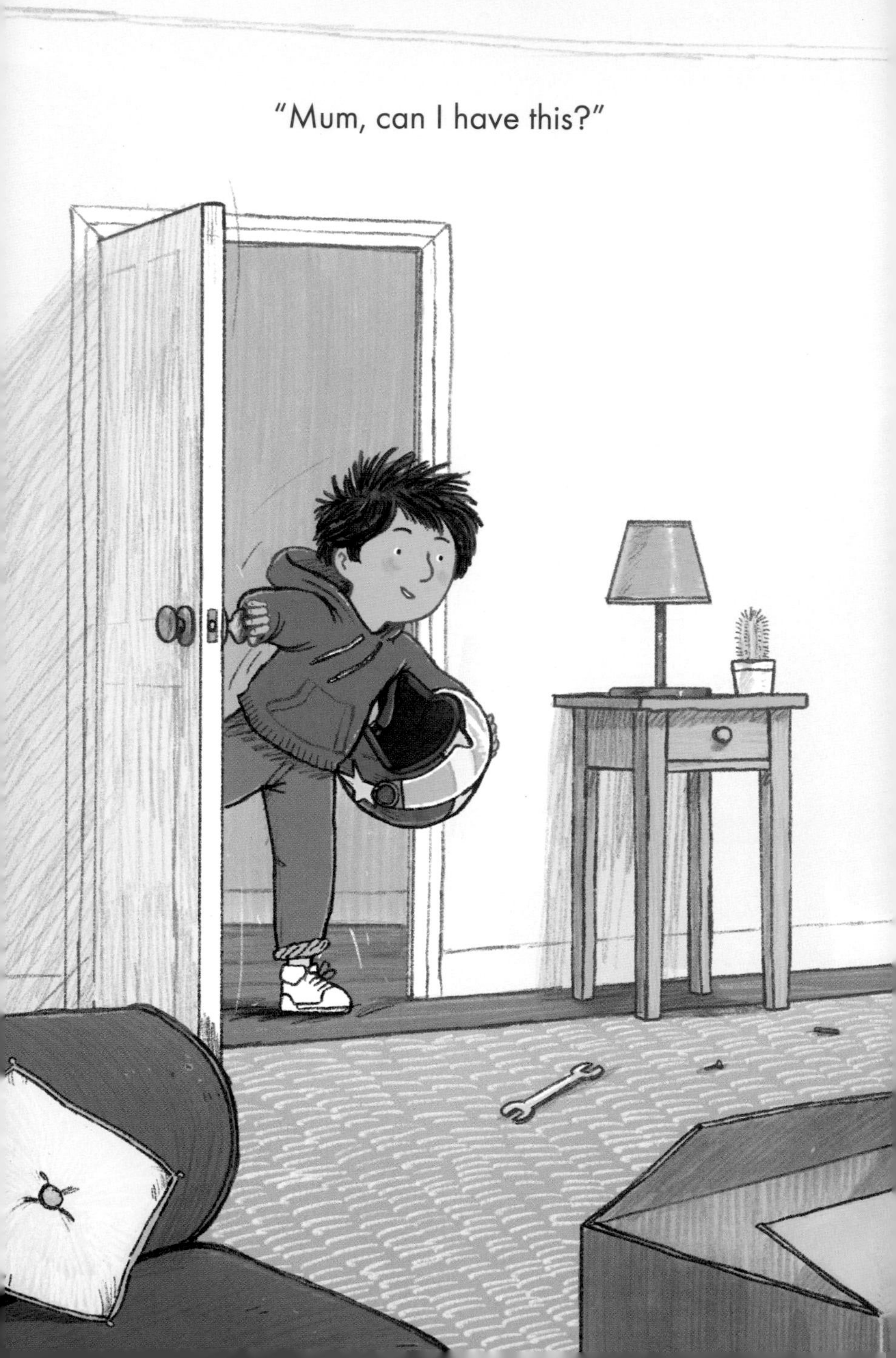

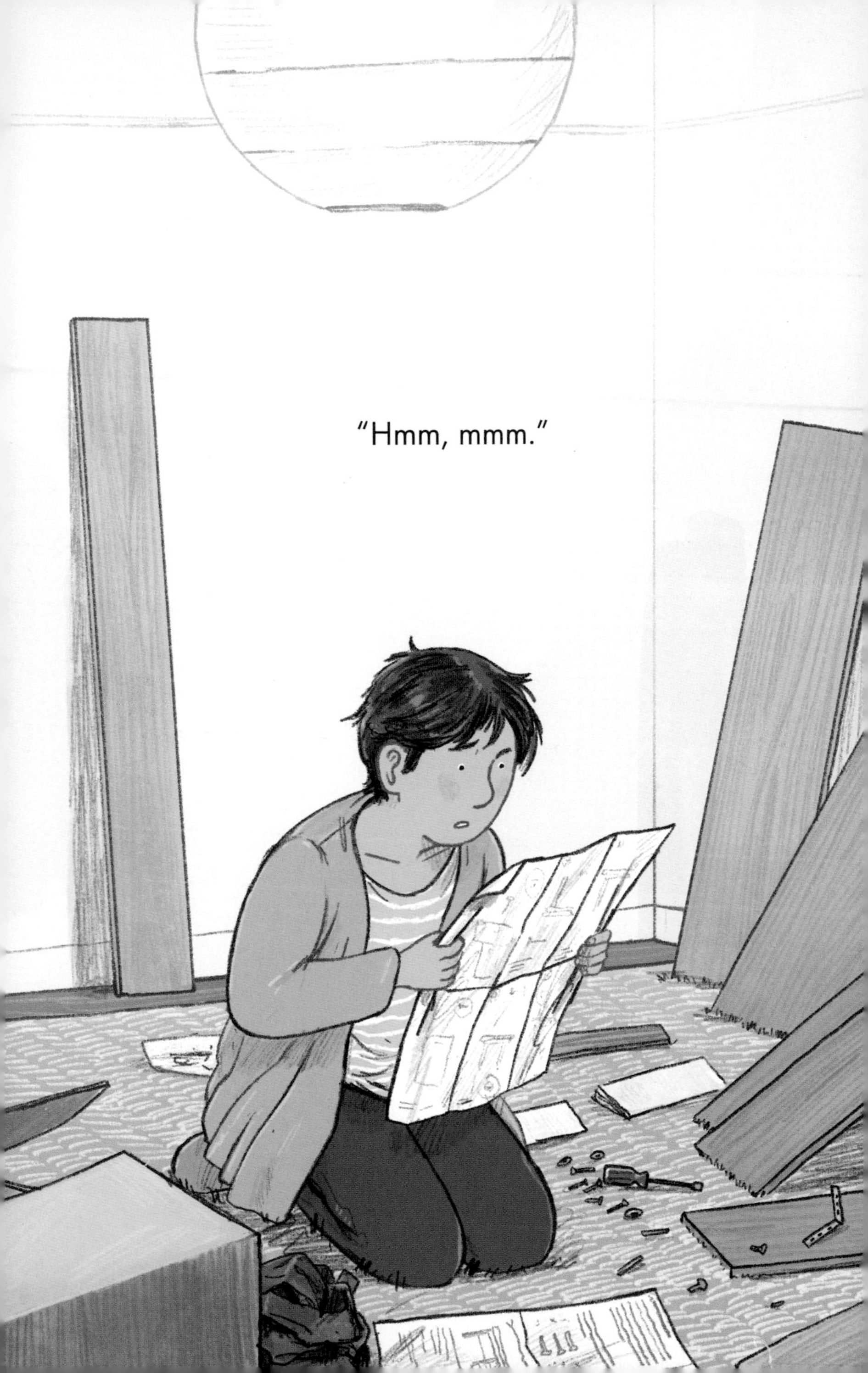
"Hmm, mmm."

"Now for some provisions," says Callum.

He studies the contents of the kitchen
cupboard then sighs. Why can't you
buy space food in the supermarket?

"And some jars for collecting samples.
Hmm..."

Callum checks his plans. "Right, now I need to connect the command module to the service module."

"Oh, Oscar! Here, let me get that off!"

"Can't you sleep somewhere else, Oscar?"

"Oscar! What have you done
with the turbo pump?"

"Almost there..."

"Ta-da! Done!"
Callum gazes up
at his creation.

"All it needs now is a name..."

"**Here we are at the launch of the Epic,**" he says in his best news reporter voice.

"*Our brave young astronaut is putting on his space helmet and boots, ready to go where no boy has gone before... Mars!*"

"The world watches with bated breath as he steps into the shuttle."

"And he's closing the hatch..."

"*Epic* to Mission Control,"
says Callum in his best astronaut
voice, strapping himself in.
"T minus one minute.
Final checks."

"Main engine start."

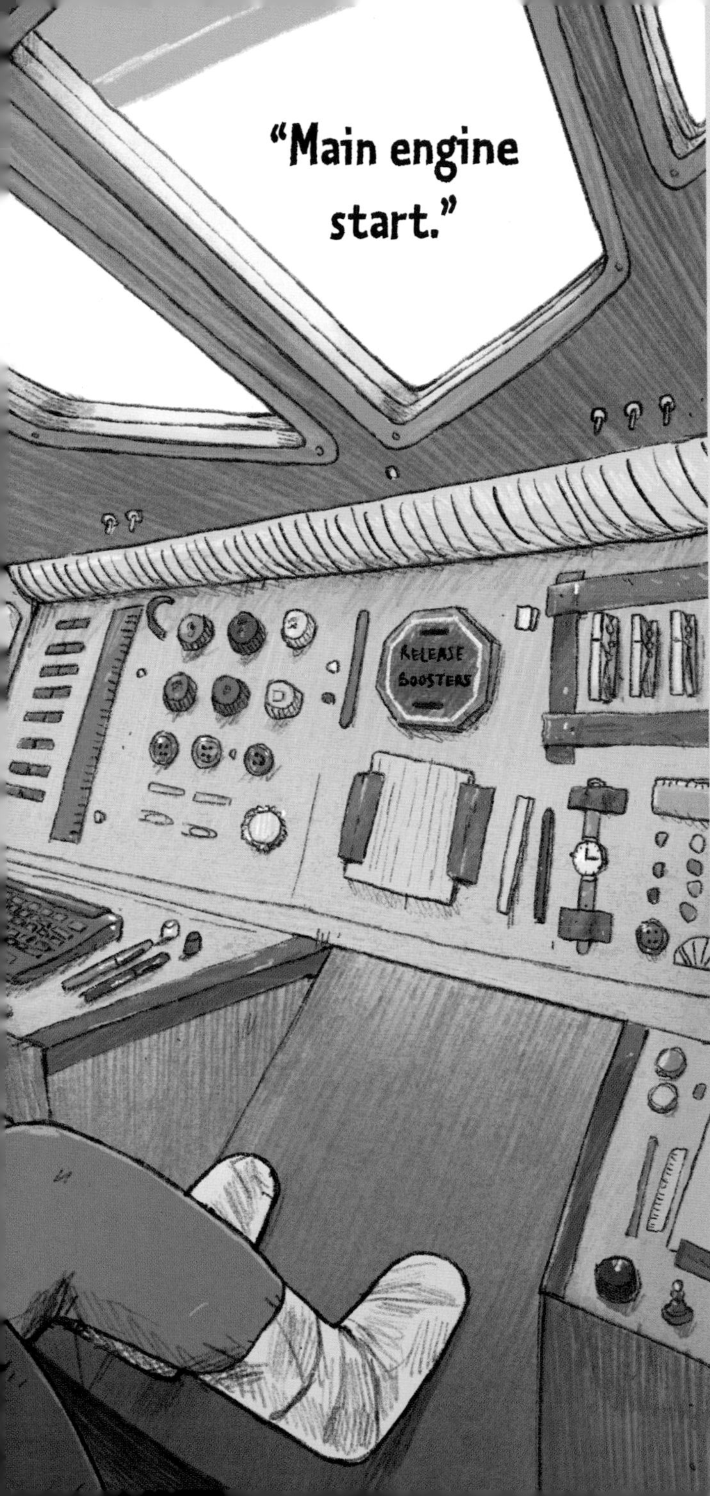
RELEASE
BOOSTERS

10

9

8

7

6

5

4

3

2

1

LIFT OFF!

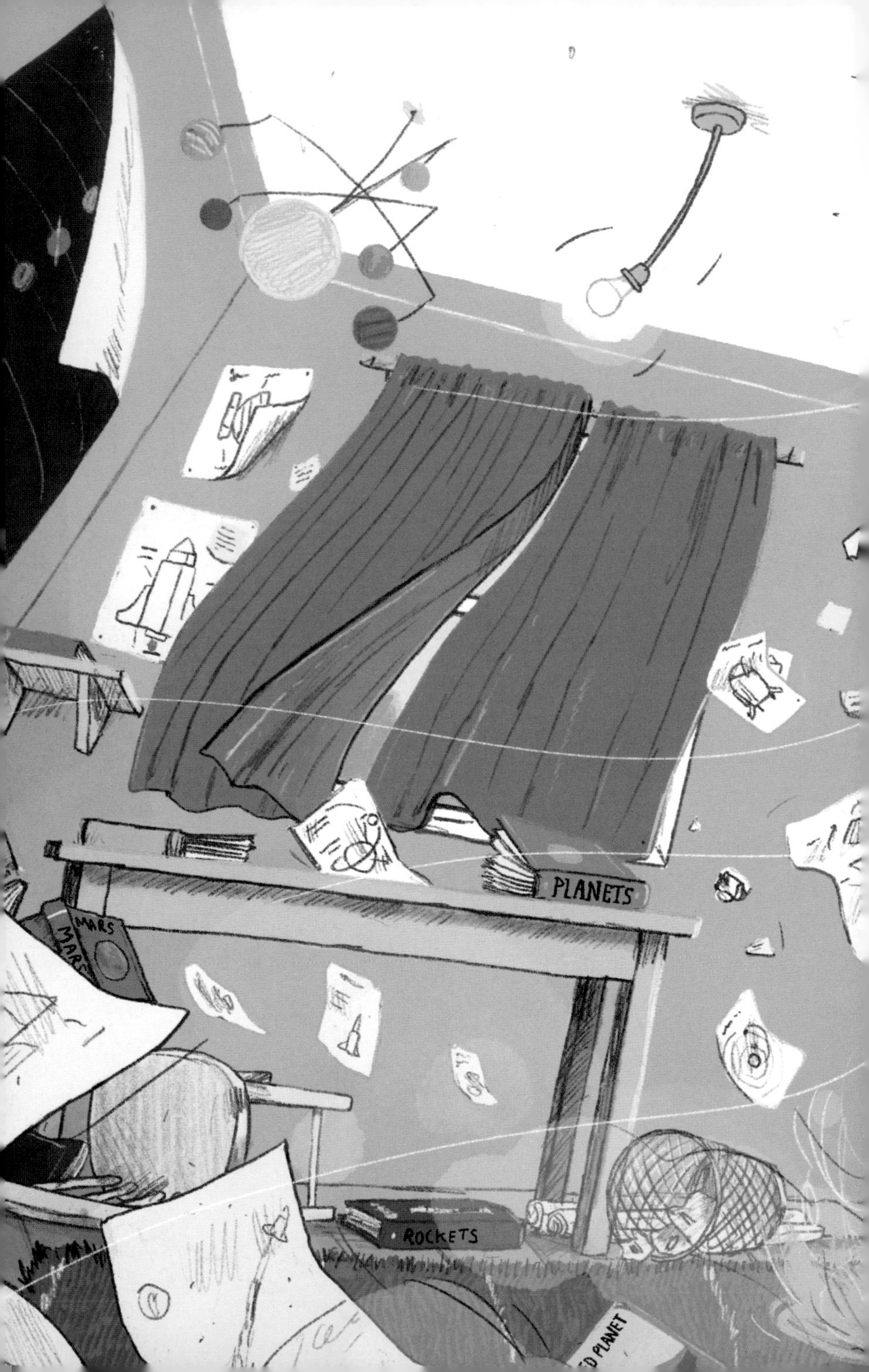
PLANETS
MARS
ROCKETS

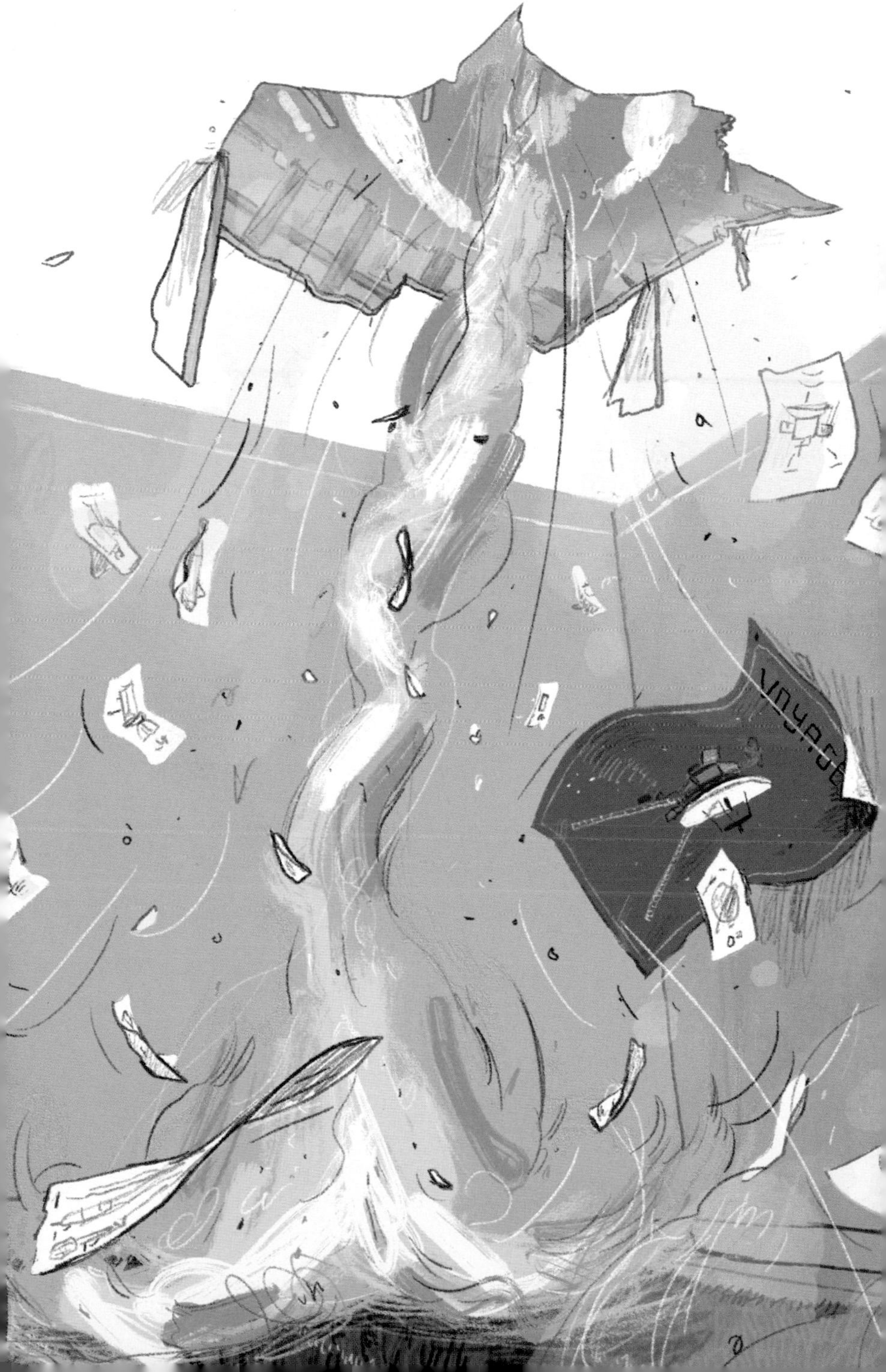

"AAAaaaAAHHH!"

Callum feels himself pushed back into the seat as if shoved by the hands of a giant.

The sky turns from light blue to blue-ish black as
the shuttle thunders higher. Then, all of a sudden,
there is TOTAL blackness.

"WOW!"

Callum switches off the engine.

"I'm the youngest person to go into space. Ever!
Now let's see if I can be the first to land on Mars."

The rocket
boosters detach
and drift away.

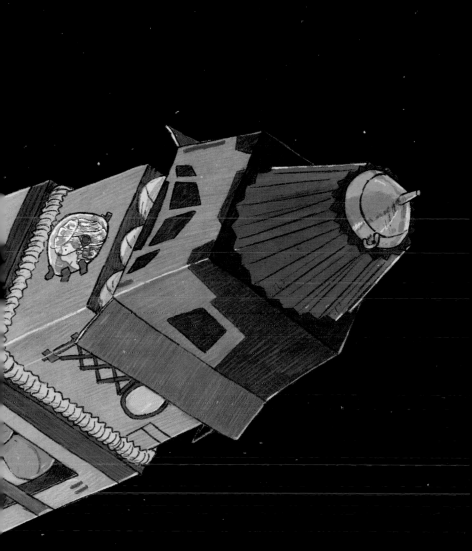

Callum gazes down at a distant Earth.
"Mission control, this is AM-A-ZING!
Where's my camera?"

He's searching for his rucksack when something brushes against the top of his head. Startled, Callum flips up his visor and looks round to see...

"HELP!" yowls Oscar.

"You can ... talk!" whispers Callum.

"In space, anything can happen," says the cat.
"Now stop yapping and get me down!"

"Hold on," says Callum.
"I'm coming!"

39

He drifts upwards ... reaches out for Oscar ...
and grabs the cat by his tail.

"*EOWWW!* Get off!" hisses Oscar, fur on end.
"What do you think I am, a balloon?"

"OK, OK!" Callum quickly lets go. "I was only trying
to get you down like you asked."

"I've changed my mind," sniffs Oscar.

"Aren't you excited about being in space?
Look at the view!" says Callum. "That reminds
me, I still need to get a photo..."

"I'm hungry," says Oscar.
"Got anything to eat?"

Callum glides down and takes his lunchbox from
his rucksack. "You can have a ham sandwich."

"No tuna? As the first cat in space,
I think I deserve better."

"But you're not the first," says Callum.
"That was a French cat called—"

"Oh, whatever!" interrupts Oscar.

Callum opens a packet of crisps but only a few make it into his mouth.

And the lemonade bubbles explode in his throat.

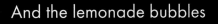

BUUUUU-RRRRP!

...until he can make out trails
of footprints.

"Those footprints were left by Neil Armstrong and Buzz Aldrin over fifty years ago," Callum tells the cat. "There's no wind on the moon, so they'll stay there forever. Awesome, huh? And over there, Oscar, that's the famous flag and—"

"It's my turn," interrupts Oscar, reaching for the controls.

"All right," says Callum. "But be—"

45

The car bashes his paw off the Turbo Boost
button and...

WHOOOSSSH!

...the shuttle blasts upwards.

"Oscar!" cries Callum.
"What have you done?
The footprints are gone!"

"Footprints aren't a good thing,"
says Oscar. "Your mum's always telling
you to wipe your feet when you come in."

"Yes, but those were— Never mind,"
says Callum. "Come on, let me take over!"

All of a sudden, flashes of red
streak past the ship like
a firework display.

"Meteor storm!" shouts Callum.
"Out of the way, cat!"

Sweat cascades down Callum's forehead and his heart thunders in his chest as he dodges the meteors. Blazing rocks whizz past the spacecraft.

Then suddenly... **KER-LUNK!**

WEEEeeeppp! WEEEeeeppp!

The emergency alarm shrieks and the console flashes like a Christmas tree.

"The fuel pipe's been hit," he groans.
"We've got no power."

Our intrepid astronaut straps on his jet pack and grabs some tools.

"Now stay here, Oscar, and touch nothing. Understood?"

"You don't want my help?" says the cat sulkily. "Fine."

Callum enters the airlock...

49

...and steps out into the infinite blackness of space.

Bang!
Bang!
Tap-**tap-tap**-tap!

"Almost done, Oscar,"
Callum reports, some time later.

Suddenly the engines power up again,
blasting Callum backwards.

"Oscar!" Callum cries, as the cord securing
him to the shuttle whips him from side to side.
"Switch off the engines. Now!"

But Oscar doesn't hear him. He's
enjoying a zero-gravity cat nap.

The cord flings Callum up against the shuttle. He grasps at the side with his fingertips and stretches up...

...but slips back down again.

Finally Callum finds a hold and scrambles
through the airlock hatch.

"I'm back!" he pants.

Oscar slowly opens one eye. "I always feel better
after a nap," he says with a yawn.

"Right..." Callum lets out a giant sigh. "If we're going to
reach Mars, we'd better get a move on. Hold on tight."

He straps himself in and reaches for
the Ultra Turbo Boost button.

WHOOOHHHOOOSShhhh!

The shuttle jolts forwards in a fierce blaze
of white light. It shivers and shudders as if it's about
to splinter into a bazillion little pieces.
Callum squeezes his eyes shut.

As the ship slows, Callum blinks his eyes open. Up ahead looms the rust-red planet.

"Mars!" Callum cries.
"No way! I did it!"

"You mean WE did it," Oscar pipes up. "You couldn't have got here without my help."

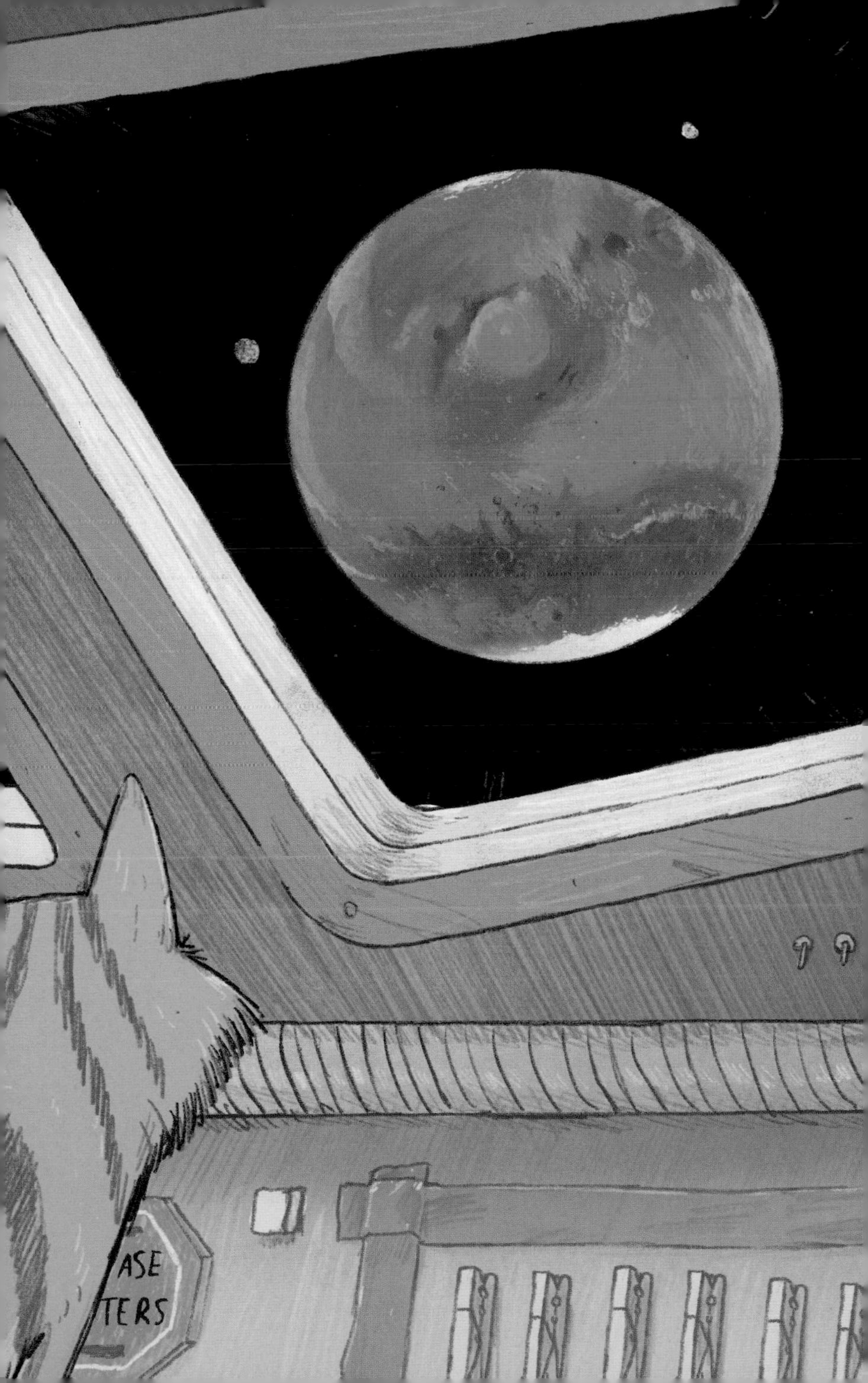
ASE
TERS

"I've got an important job for you, Oscar,"
Callum says as he clambers down into the
landing module. "I need you to stay here
and look after the shuttle."

Oscar narrows his eyes. "Very well," he says,
to Callum's surprise. Then he stretches and
gives a dramatic yawn.

Buuu-dump!

The landing module detaches.

It touches down.

Callum flings open the hatch and stands at the top of the metal steps. The Martian wind whips around him. *This is it,* he thinks. *I'm about to be the first—*

Just then he feels something brush against his leg. He looks down to see Oscar bounding towards the surface of the red planet.

"Oscar? You were supposed to stay on the–"

"I'm first. I won! I won!" cries Oscar. "Winner winner, chicken dinner. Mmm, chicken." He licks his lips. "Don't suppose we'll find anything decent to eat around here."

Callum rolls his eyes, then steps down to join the cat. "You never know... Let's explore!"

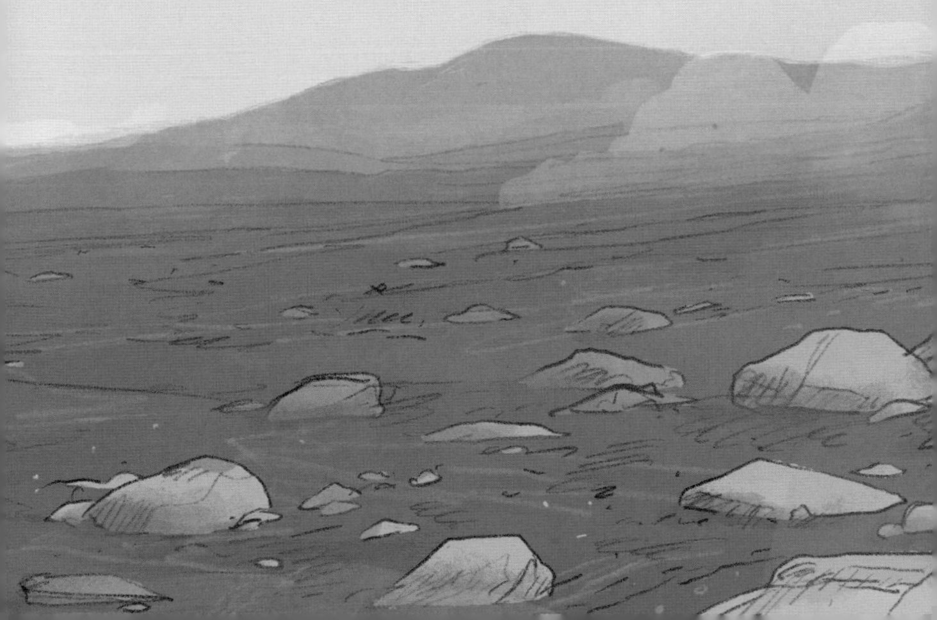

Together they bound across the craggy ground, leaping up over boulders and down into craters.

From time to time, Callum stops to take a sample of rock.

From time to time, Oscar pauses to shake the dust from his paws.

"Look," says Callum, catching sight of a
vehicle up ahead.

"What's that?"
asks Oscar.

"*Curiosity*," answers Callum. "It's a rover that sends
back footage and data to the scientists at NASA."

"We could hitch a lift,"
suggests Oscar.

"I don't think so!" Callum laughs as the vehicle
crawls slowly past. "Come on, this way!" he says.

By the time Callum reaches the dunes, Oscar is trailing way behind. The nearest dunes are like waves lapping against the shore, while in the distance they rise up like a tsunami.

"Keep up, Oscar!" calls Callum.

"How many of these things are there?"
gasps the cat as they clamber up the side
of a massive dune.

"This is the last one, promise," says Callum.
"Just think how much fun it'll be to slide
down the other side."

"You ready?" says Callum when Oscar joins him at last. "Three, two, one—"

"Woohoo!"

Oscar leaps after him, claws outstretched... And lands right in the middle of Callum's stomach.

"I quite enjoyed that," says Oscar, jumping off at the bottom.

"I bet," mutters Callum.

Later still...

"My paws ache," whines Oscar. "Carry me!"

"I'm not carrying you!"

"Well, I'm not walking any further."

"Go back to the landing module then!"
snaps Callum. "I told you not to come."

"Fine," says Oscar, turning tail.

Callum heads on alone.

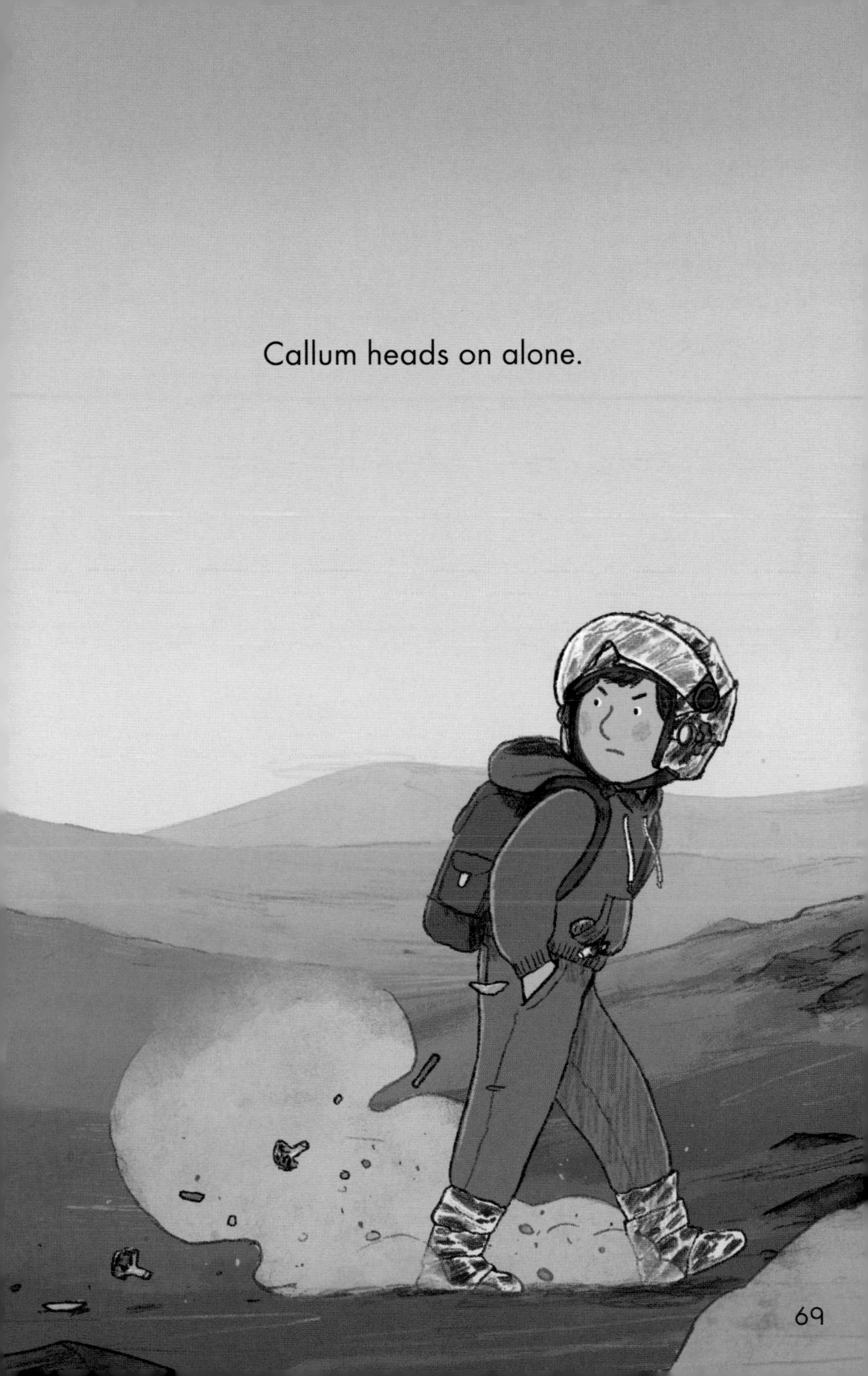

Finally Callum reaches a broad channel,
which stretches in both directions
as far as he can see.

"The Valles Marineris!" he cries.
"It's five times deeper than Earth's Grand Canyon!
How cool is that?"

He looks down to see Oscar's reaction –
but then remembers the cat is no longer with him.

Callum notices it growing colder.
The sun is beginning to set.

"A Martian sunset!" he whispers,
and he watches the blue sphere sink
towards the horizon.

As the sun disappears, Callum turns
to head back to the landing module.
But something very strange
has happened...

"Woah! What on Mars is that...?"

To his astonishment, where before
there was dusty red rock he now
sees a soaring emerald jungle.

As he reaches to snip a sample from a nearby plant, he feels something brush against his ankle.

"What the—?"

A thorny shoot loops around Callum's legs, then slithers upwards and coils itself round his body, like a python squeezing its prey. He desperately tries to wriggle his way free but it pulls him to the ground and drags him across the jungle floor.

"Help!" he splutters as a giant pea pod looms over him.

The pod opens up, revealing rows of teeth...

Suddenly there's a swish of claws. **KATCHA!**

Followed by a sequence of vicious swipes.
KATCHA! KATCHA!

Oscar slices through
the stalk of the pod and
Callum plummets to the
ground.

"OOF!"

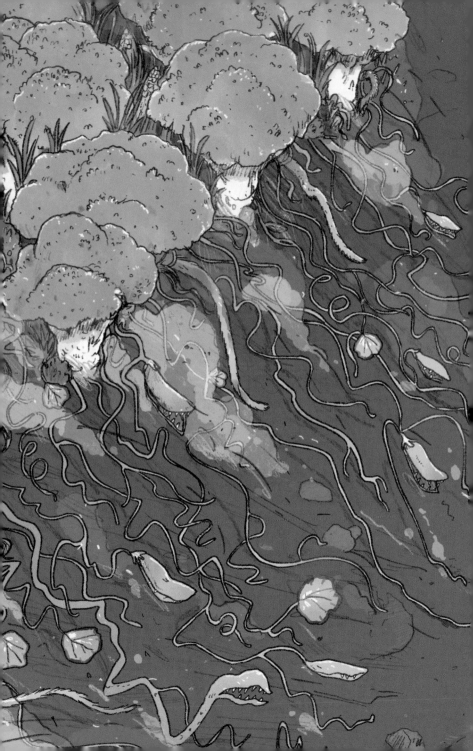

Together the pair fight their way through
the jungle...

Dash up and down the dunes...

Leap over boulders and craters...

And sprint for the landing module...

"That ... was ... close," gasps Callum,
slamming the hatch door shut behind them.

But as he powers up the landing module
it begins to wobble and shake.

"What's happening?" Callum yells.
"Why aren't we moving?"

Oscar slams his paw on the throttle
and the module shoots up towards the shuttle.

Once they're safely on board,
Oscar turns to Callum.

"Well, aren't you going to thank me
for rescuing you?"

"As soon as we're home, I'll give you
some tuna," promises Callum.

"I think I deserve a whole tin," says
Oscar. "But make sure you keep
the juice. That's the best bit!"

Oscar licks his paws.

Callum is about to set a course for home when—

"What is it?" cries Callum. "What's wrong?"

"My paws, they taste of broccoli! Bleeugh!"

Callum...
Mission control to
Callum! Come in,
Callum...

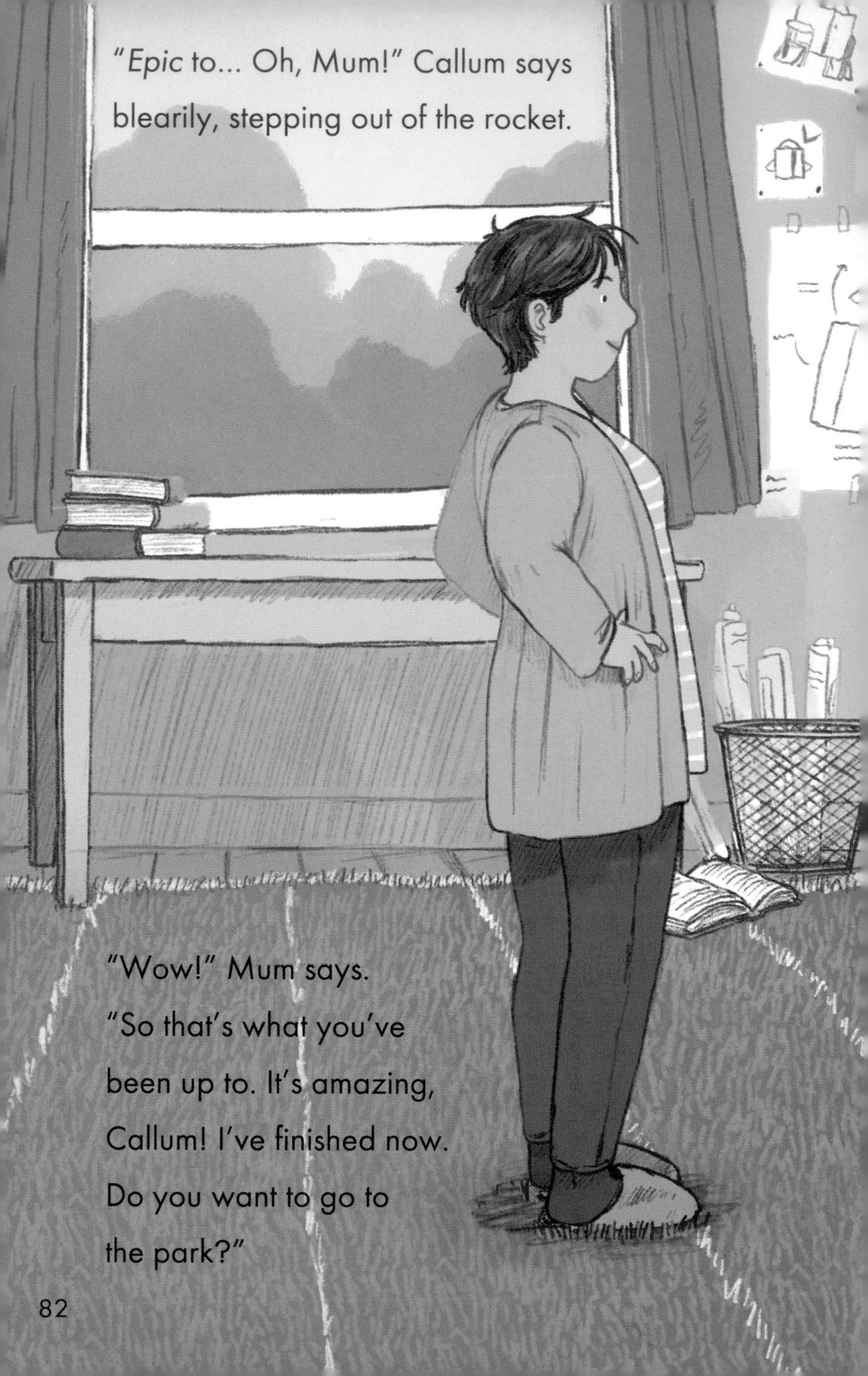

"*Epic* to... Oh, Mum!" Callum says blearily, stepping out of the rocket.

"Wow!" Mum says. "So that's what you've been up to. It's amazing, Callum! I've finished now. Do you want to go to the park?"

"Sure," says Callum.
"Can I just give Oscar
some tuna first?"

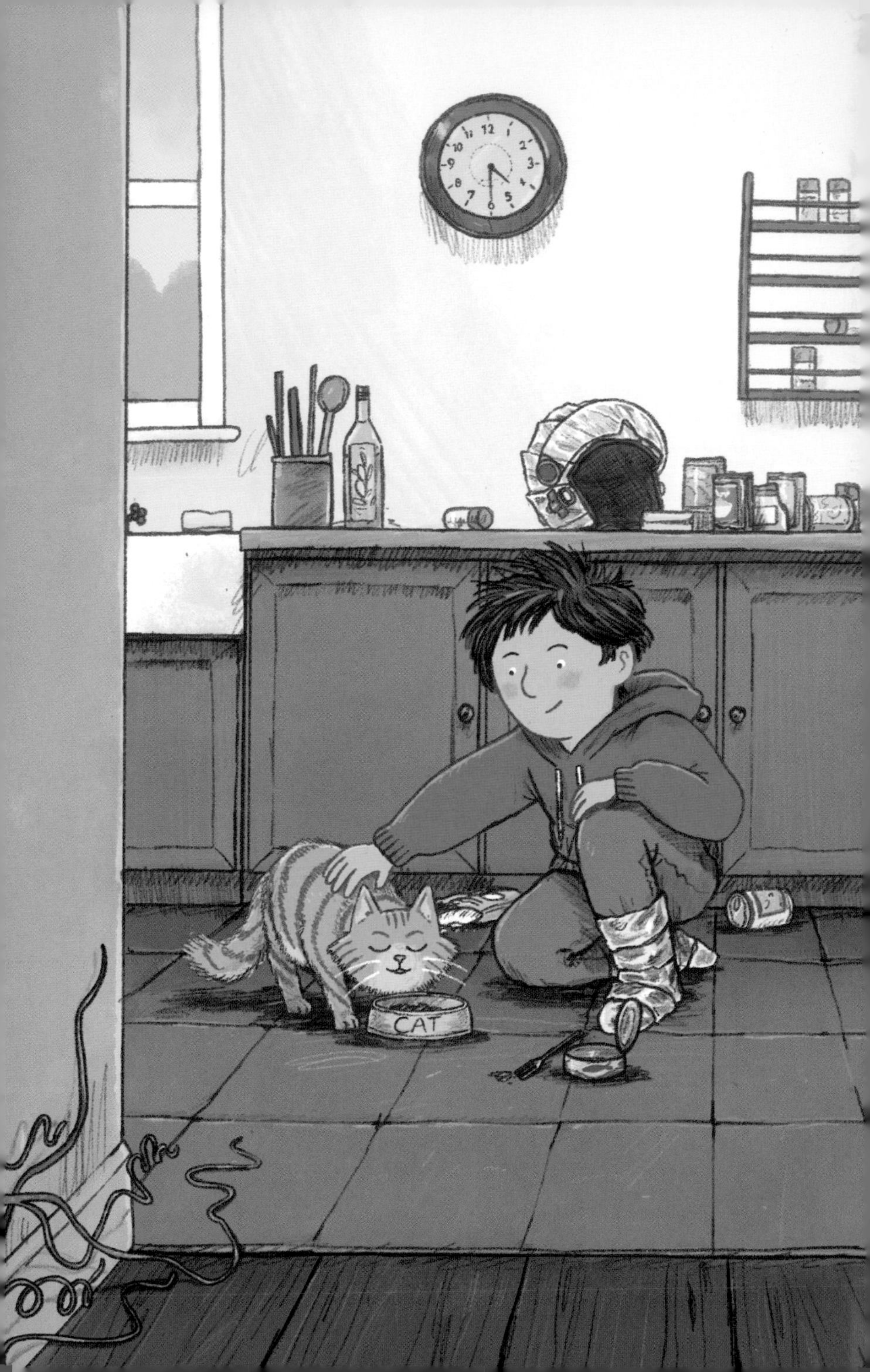
CAT

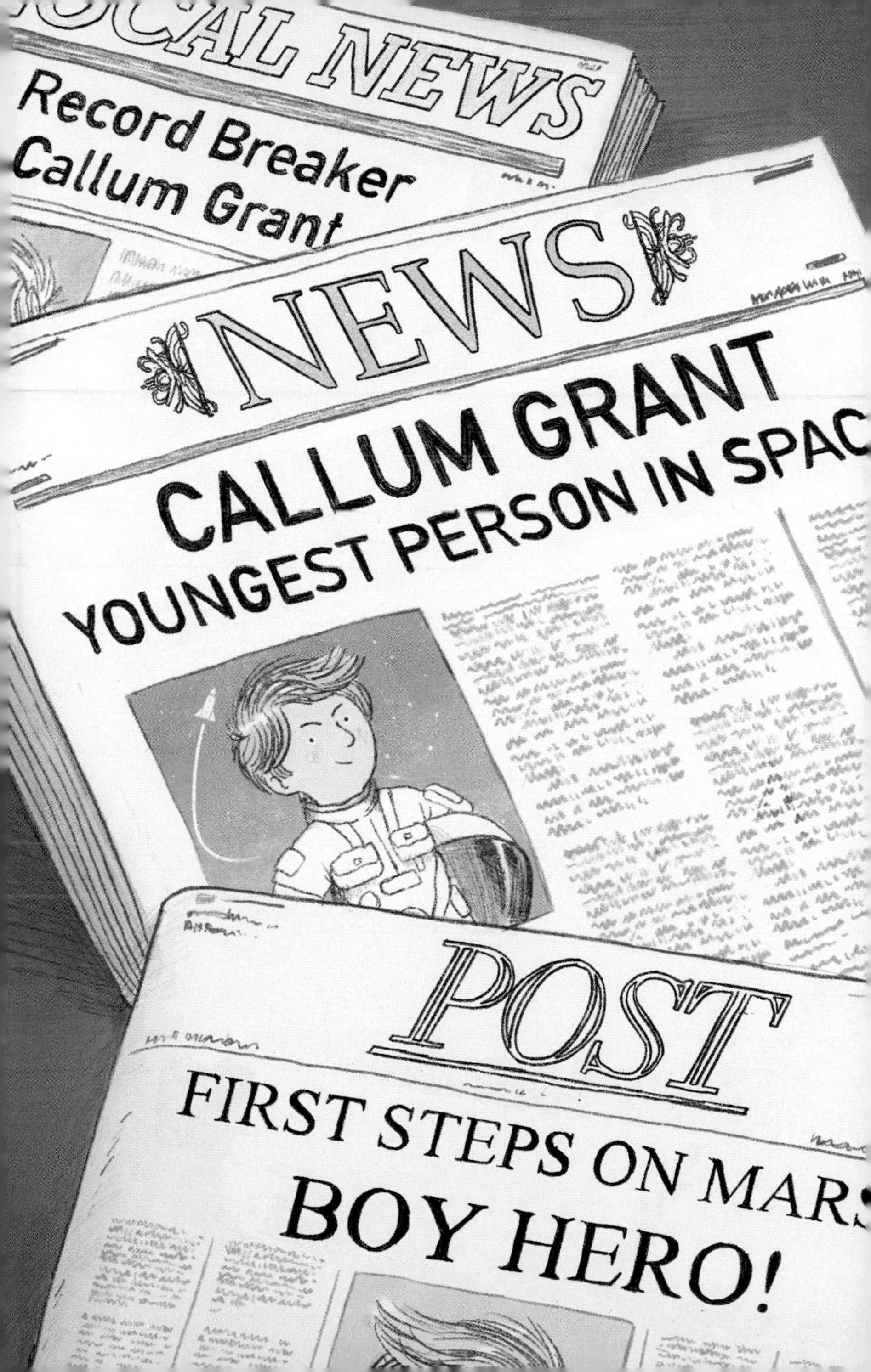
LOCAL NEWS
Record Breaker Callum Grant
NEWS
CALLUM GRANT
YOUNGEST PERSON IN SPAC
POST
FIRST STEPS ON MARS
BOY HERO!